A NOTE TO PARENTS

When your children are ready to "step into reading," giving them the right books is as crucial as giving them the right food to eat. **Step into Reading Books** present exciting stories and information reinforced with lively, colorful illustrations that make learning to read fun, satisfying, and worthwhile. They are priced so that acquiring an entire library of them is affordable. And they are beginning readers with a difference—they're written on five levels.

Early Step into Reading Books are designed for brand-new readers, with large type and only one or two lines of very simple text per page. **Step 1 Books** feature the same easy-to-read type as the **Early Step into Reading Books**, but with more words per page. **Step 2 Books** are both longer and slightly more difficult, while **Step 3 Books** introduce readers to paragraphs and fully developed plot lines. **Step 4 Books** offer exciting nonfiction for the increasingly independent reader.

The grade levels assigned to the five steps—preschool through kindergarten for the Early Books, preschool through grade 1 for Step 1, grades 1 through 3 for Step 2, grades 2 through 3 for Step 3, and grades 2 through 4 for Step 4—are intended only as guides. Some children move through all five steps very rapidly; others climb the steps over a period of several years. Either way, these books will help your child "step into reading" in style!

For Mara, a little mermaid in Santa Monica

Copyright © 1996 Big Tuna Trading Company, LLC.
CRITTERS OF THE NIGHT™ and all prominent characters featured in this book and
the distinctive likenesses thereof are trademarks of Big Tuna Trading Company, LLC.
All rights reserved under International and Pan-American Copyright Conventions.
Published in the United States by Random House, Inc., New York, and
simultaneously in Canada by Random House of Canada Limited, Toronto.

http://www.randomhouse.com/

Library of Congress Cataloging-in-Publication Data
Mayer, Mercer.
Kiss of the mermaid / written by Erica Farber and J. R. Sansevere.
     p. cm. — (Mercer Mayer's critters of the night) (Step into reading. A step 3 book)
SUMMARY: When Vavooka turns all of the merpeople into stone, Thistle hopes to secure
their release by winning a chess game against the evil sea witch.
ISBN 0-679-87381-3 (trade) — ISBN 0-679-97381-8 (lib. bdg.)
[1. Mermaids—Fiction. 2. Magic—Fiction. 3. Chess—Fiction.]
I. Farber, Erica. II. Sansevere, John R. III. Title. IV. Series: Mayer, Mercer. Critters of the night.
V. Series: Step into reading. Step 3 book.
PZ7.F2275Ki 1996
[Fic]—dc20 96-11066

Printed in the United States of America   10 9 8 7 6 5 4 3 2
STEP INTO READING is a trademark of Random House, Inc.

 A BIG TUNA TRADING COMPANY, LLC/J. R. SANSEVERE BOOK

Step into Reading™

MERCER MAYER'S
CRITTERS OF THE NIGHT™

KISS OF THE MERMAID

Written by
Erica Farber and J. R. Sansevere

A Step 3 Book

Random House 🏠 New York

Wanda   Jack   Thistle   Axel

Bones

Snake

Capt. Short Bob   Dracul Duck   Wolf Mouse

Groad　　　　**Frankengator**　　　　**Moose Mummy**

Uncle Mole　　　**Zombie Mombie**　　　**Auntie Bell**

1
The Kiss

Every night, Thistle Howl and Moose Mummy played chess.

While they played, they listened to the mermaids singing.

The mermaids liked to sing on a rock in the middle of the swamp.

That is why the rock was called Mermaid Rock.

One night, a big storm blew up.

The wind and the rain were so loud that Moose Mummy and Thistle couldn't hear the mermaids singing.

Moose Mummy moved his king. Thistle moved her queen.

"Checkmate!" said Thistle.

Moose Mummy sighed. He just couldn't beat Thistle. She always won. She was the best chess player around.

Suddenly, the storm got much worse.

"BOOM! BOOM!" Big claps of thunder seemed to shake the room.

"CRACK! CRACK!" Blinding flashes of lightning lit up the sky.

Thistle and Moose Mummy looked out the window. Their eyes opened wide.

One little mermaid sat all by herself on Mermaid Rock.

"Where have the other mermaids gone? And why isn't she singing?" asked Thistle.

"I don't know," said Moose Mummy. "But I'm not going out there to find out. It's too scary."

"I'm not afraid," said Thistle. She put
on her boots and raincoat and ran outside
to Mermaid Rock.

The lone little mermaid was crying.

"Why are you crying?" said Thistle.

The little mermaid looked at Thistle. A
tear dripped down her cheek.

"My parents and my sisters and all of

my friends who live under the sea have
been put under a terrible spell," she said
with a sob. "You see, I'm a mermaid
princess. My name is Mara."

"My name is Thistle," said Thistle.
"What kind of spell are they under?"

"Vavooka, the evil sea witch, has
turned them to stone," said Mara.

Then she began to cry all over again.

"If only I were a mermaid!" said
Thistle. "I would go to the bottom of the
sea and help you. But I'm just a girl.
I can't swim under the sea. I don't have
a mermaid tail like you."

"That's easy to fix," said Mara.

She kissed Thistle on the cheek . . . and
before you could say "Splish! Splash!"
Thistle turned into a mermaid!

2

The Sea Witch

Down . . . down . . . down . . . they went,
deeper and deeper into the sea.

They whirred and whizzed through the water. Faster and faster they swam.

Finally, they came to the bottom. In front of them was a big dark cave.

Mara put her finger to her lips. "Shh!" she whispered.

Mara quickly swam behind a clump of seaweed. Thistle swam beside her.

"That's where Vavooka lives," Mara said. "In that creepy cave. There's an impossible maze inside. And there are horrible creatures that bite and pinch."

Thistle looked into the cave.

"Don't worry," she said. "I'm not scared of a cave or a maze or even creatures that bite and pinch."

Thistle swam toward the cave.

Suddenly, something big and slimy swam out of the cave.

"Look out!" yelled Mara.

There, before Thistle, was a huge sea monster!

The sea monster held up his sword.
"Who goes there?" he said.
"Thistle Howl," said Thistle.
"Off with your head!" said the sea monster.
"Swim!" Mara yelled at Thistle. "Or the sea monster will chop off your head and Vavooka will eat you for dinner."
Thistle looked right into the sea monster's eyes.

"I'm not afraid of you!" she said.

"But I'm a sea monster," said the sea monster. "Everyone under the sea is afraid of me. That is why I am called a sea monster!

"GRRRRR!" he growled.

Thistle shook her head.

"That's not a very scary growl," she said.

"Really?" said the sea monster.

"Really," said Thistle.

The sea monster hung his head low.

"Don't be sad," said Thistle. "You can help us."

"I can?" said the sea monster. "I never helped anybody before."

"This is Mara, the mermaid princess," said Thistle. "She's looking for her family and all her friends. Vavooka turned them to stone. They're somewhere in the cave."

As soon as the sea monster heard the name "Vavooka," his eyes opened wide.

"She's a meanie," said the sea monster. "The biggest meanie in the sea. And she said she would turn me into sea foam if I let anyone enter her cave."

"Leave it to me," said Thistle. "I won't let her turn you into sea foam. Just show us the way through the maze."

The sea monster led them into the cave.
It was dark and damp and dreary.
Little creatures gnashed their teeth and snapped their claws.
But Thistle wasn't scared.
"Stop that!" she scolded. "It's rude!"
The creatures all looked at Thistle in surprise. They stopped gnashing and

snapping at once. No one had ever yelled at them before.

"Thank you," said Thistle.

Thistle and Mara followed the sea monster down a long hallway. And then another one. And another. And another.

Finally, they came to a big door made of sea glass.

"Where are we?" asked Thistle.

"We're in the center of the maze," said the sea monster. "This is Sea Glass Hall, where Vavooka lives."

"Oooh," said Mara. "I don't want to go in there. I'm scared."

"Me too," said the sea monster.

"Don't be scared," said Thistle.

She turned the crystal doorknob on the sea-glass door.

Then, hand in hand, the three of them swam into Sea Glass Hall . . .

All along the hall were doors.

All the doors were closed except for one. Through the open door, Thistle, Mara, and the sea monster saw a room that was filled with stone statues.

"Look!" cried Mara. "Here are my parents, my sisters, and all my friends."

Thistle, Mara, and the sea monster swam into the room.

"That's strange," said Thistle. "All the statues look like giant chess pieces. And the floor looks like a giant chessboard."

"Stop right there!" shouted an evil-sounding voice.

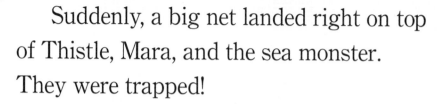

Suddenly, a big net landed right on top of Thistle, Mara, and the sea monster. They were trapped!

"Ha, ha, ha!" cackled Vavooka, the evil sea witch. "No one can fool me," she said. "Especially silly little children. All evil witches can smell children miles away.

We have the best noses in the whole world."

"And the biggest, too," said Thistle.
"I'm not afraid of you!"

"Well, you should be," said Vavooka.
"Because I'm going to turn all three of you
to stone before you can say 'Splish! Splash!'"

3

Magic Wands

Suddenly, there was a crashing sound.

Something stormed through the wall of Sea Glass Hall.

It was a big mermaid riding an electric broom.

It was none other than Thistle's Auntie Bell.

"Auntie Bell!" cried Thistle. "When did you turn into a mermaid?"

"Tonight!" said Auntie Bell. "I'm here to help you. Leave everything to me."

"Well, well, well," said Vavooka. "If it isn't good witch Bell!"

"Ooka, ooka, ooka," said Auntie Bell. "If it isn't bad witch Vavooka!"

The two witches faced off. They pulled out their magic wands.

Vavooka pointed her magic wand at Auntie Bell and said:

"Abracadabra!
Swish! Swish! Swish!
Turn good witch Bell
Into a stinky fish!"

"You can't do that!" yelled Thistle.

But it was too late. Before their eyes, Auntie Bell turned into a big orange fish!

Her magic wand fell to the floor. It rolled under Vavooka's big black pot of nasty, bubbling witch's brew.

"Glub, glub, glub," bubbled the big orange fish that had once been Auntie Bell.

"Oh, no!" gasped Mara. "We're doomed."

Vavooka laughed her evil laugh. She turned to Thistle and her friends. "Kiss your nasty little lives good-bye," Vavooka said. She raised her magic wand.

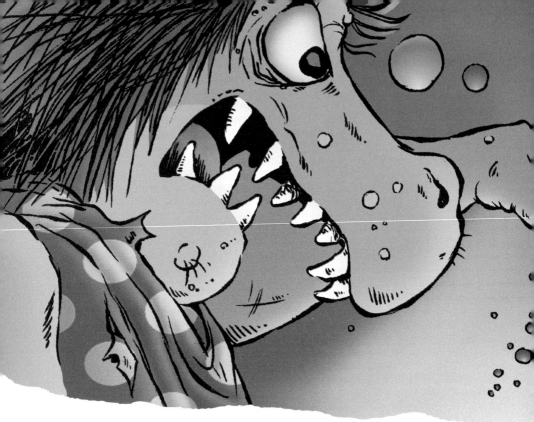

Thistle's eyes darted every which way, in search of help. She looked around the room at the statues and the black and yellow squares on the floor. Suddenly, it came to her. She knew what she had to do!

"Wait!" she cried. "I have one last wish."

"Fie on your wish!" said Vavooka.

"Please!" said Thistle. "All prisoners are allowed one last wish!"

"Oh, all right," said Vavooka. "What is your wish?"

"Let me out first," said Thistle. "And then I will tell you."

"Be careful," whispered Mara.

"Very careful," added the sea monster. He nodded his big sea monster head up and down.

Vavooka lifted the net off Thistle. "Now, what is your wish?" she asked.

"I wish to challenge you to a game of chess," said Thistle.

"Chess?" said Vavooka. Her red eyes gleamed. "I love playing chess."

"I know," said Thistle.

"In fact, I'm planning to turn you and your little friends into pawns. I need more for my chess collection," said Vavooka. She pointed to the stone statues.

"Oh, no!" screamed Mara and the sea monster.

Vavooka laughed her evil laugh. "Look at the purple king and queen," she said.

"Those are my parents," said Mara with a sob.

"Not anymore," said Vavooka.

"If I win, you will have to take your evil spell off all the statues and off my Auntie Bell," said Thistle. "You will have to turn them all back the way they were."

"And if I win?" asked Vavooka, picking a piece of food from between her teeth.

"If you win, then you can turn the three of us to stone," said Thistle.

"Oh, no!" screamed Mara and the sea monster again.

"Okay," said Vavooka. "I'll play."

"Do you promise to take your evil spell off everyone if I win?" asked Thistle.

"I promise," said Vavooka. "But I am the best chess player under the sea. You will never win."

"Let the game begin," said Thistle.

4

Checkmate

Thistle and Vavooka looked at the black and yellow squares on the floor.

"I'll be purple," said Vavooka. "You be green."

"Okay," said Thistle.

"I go first," said Vavooka. "Since it's my house."

Vavooka pointed her magic wand. A purple knight floated up into the air. It landed on a black square.

Thistle studied the chessboard. This
wasn't easy. She was so small and the
chess pieces were so large. Finally, she
decided to move a green pawn. She had to
push as hard as she could to move it. Stone
pawns are very heavy, especially when
they are bigger than you are.

Thistle and Vavooka took turns making their moves.

The game of chess went on and on.

Mara and the sea monster began to worry. But Thistle was a good match for Vavooka. Thistle was beginning to get tired, though. Moving giant stone pieces around is hard work.

Finally, Vavooka had Thistle's king surrounded.

"Check!" called Vavooka. "I win!"

Thistle smiled. "No, you don't," she said. She made another move. And the game continued.

"I'm still going to win," said Vavooka after a few more moves.

"No, you're not," said Thistle. "You fell right into my trap."

It was the same trap that always worked on Moose Mummy. Thistle moved her king. And there, right behind her king, was her queen.

"Checkmate!" called Thistle. "I win! Now you have to take your evil spell off everyone and turn them back the way they were."

Thistle smiled at her friends.

"Hooray!" shouted Mara and the sea monster.

"Glub! Glub!" bubbled the big orange fish that had once been Auntie Bell.

But Vavooka had other ideas. She laughed her evil laugh. She raised her magic wand and pointed it at Thistle, Mara, and the sea monster.

"Get ready for an eternal life of stone," she hissed.

"What do you mean?" said Thistle. "A deal's a deal. I won fair and square."

"And we saw it!" said Mara.

"We sure did!" added the sea monster.

"So what?" hissed Vavooka.

"You promised," said Thistle.

"I had my fingers crossed," said Vavooka. "So it doesn't count."

"That's cheating," said Thistle.

"All evil sea witches cheat. Didn't you know that?" said Vavooka.

"Oh, no!" gasped Mara.

The sea monster sniffled.

"Bye-bye!" said Vavooka.

She waved her magic wand.

At that very instant, Thistle knocked over the big black pot of bubbling brew.

It covered Vavooka from head to toe with green goo.

"Aahh!" screamed Vavooka as the green goo hardened.

And before their eyes, Vavooka turned into an ugly green statue with a long green nose, red eyes, and sharp, pointy teeth.

Thistle pulled the net off Mara and the sea monster.

Then she picked up Auntie Bell's magic wand. She waved the wand over the big orange fish. Then she said this spell:

"Fishy swimming
In the sea,
Now a mermaid
You shall be!"

Suddenly, the big orange fish turned back into Auntie Bell.

"Hooray!" shouted Thistle, Mara, and the sea monster.

"But how do we turn the statues back?" Thistle asked Auntie Bell.

"Is there a special spell?" asked Mara.

"Will you do it?" asked the sea monster.

"I can't," said Auntie Bell. "Only Mara can do it."

"Me?" said Mara. "But I'm just a mermaid princess. I don't know any magic spells."

"You don't need a magic spell," said Auntie Bell.

"But without a spell I don't have any power," said Mara.

"Yes, you do," said Auntie Bell. "Give each statue a kiss. One kiss is better than any magic spell."

Mara swam up to her parents, the purple king and queen. She kissed the queen on the cheek. And all at once the queen turned back into a mermaid!

Thistle and the sea monster cheered. Auntie Bell smiled.

Mara kissed the king on the cheek. And suddenly the king turned back into a merman!

As fast as she could, Mara kissed all of the chess pieces on the cheek. And one by one, they all turned back into merpeople.

The merpeople danced for joy!

Auntie Bell and Thistle said good-bye.
Then they hopped onto Auntie Bell's
broom and headed back home.

They got there just as the sun was
beginning to rise. And before they knew it,
their mermaid tails disappeared.

The mermaids rose up out of the water.
They smiled as they sang their new song:

"We thank you, Thistle,
And Auntie Bell, too,
With a big 'Splish! Splash!'
From us to you.
We want you to know
From now to the end,
We'll always be
Your best mermaid friends!"